# HOT SUVS

# RANGE ROVER SV AUTOBIOGRAPHY LWB

Charles Piddock

rourkeeducationalmedia.com

**HOT SUVS**  RANGE ROVER SV AUTOBIOGRAPHY LWB

## TABLE OF CONTENTS

Number One ........................................................... 5
Power Under the Hood ................................. 6
Inner Beauty ........................................................ 8
Button Power .................................................... 10
Air Power ............................................................. 14
Rugged Ride ..................................................... 16
All Seeing ............................................................ 20
Parking Pro ........................................................ 22

The Range Rover Story ............................... 24
Electrifying Future ...................................... 29
Glossary ....................................................... 30
Index ............................................................ 31
Show What You Know ............................... 31
Further Reading ......................................... 31
About the Author ....................................... 32

## HOT SUVS — RANGE ROVER SV AUTOBIOGRAPHY LWB

# NUMBER ONE

What is the No. 1 sport utility vehicle (SUV) on the market today? Many auto fans say it is the Range Rover SV Autobiography LWB. The Range Rover SV is simply more powerful and more luxurious than its main competitors.

Range Rover is a famous British auto maker. *SV* stands for "special vehicle." *Autobiography* implies owning one says good things about the owner. *LWB* stands for "long wheel base."

The Range Rover SV Autobiography LWB is the most luxurious and powerful Range Rover ever produced in the model's 45-year history.

# Power Under the Hood

The Range Rover SV Autobiography LWB has stand-out looks and road-crunching power to go with them. Beneath its hood, like a crouching tiger, is a big V-8 engine ready to roar. The engine produces 550 **horsepower** and 502 pound-feet (680.6 Newton-meters) of **torque**. That gives the Range Rover SV Autobiography LWB about five times the horsepower and five times the torque of an average car.

The more torque a vehicle has, the better it can accelerate from a stop and the more strength it has for towing.

# RANGE ROVER SV AUTOBIOGRAPHY LWB     HOT SUVS

The Range Rover's powerful engine looks as cool as the SUV's body style.

HOT SUVS     RANGE ROVER SV AUTOBIOGRAPHY LWB

# INNER BEAUTY

The cabin of a Range Rover SV Autobiography is not what you might expect in a rugged four-wheel drive SUV that can conquer the toughest **terrain**. It's more like entering a **stylish** room trimmed with expensive leather. The cabin has soft leather seats, leather panels on its inside doors, and leather trim on the dashboard and elsewhere. Even the **cargo** area is leather.

> Much of the leather and polished wood trim in the Range Rover SV is crafted at Range Rover's Special Vehicle Operations in Great Britain.

HOT SUVS    RANGE ROVER SV AUTOBIOGRAPHY LWB

# BUTTON POWER

Once inside the Range Rover SV, you don't need to turn any levers. All you have to do is push buttons. Press a button to adjust the seats. Press a button to open up portable trays on both sides to hold your laptop or tablet.

As driver and passengers sit in the Range Rover SV, each can adjust the temperature through four separate climate-control zones. In addition, soft interior lighting gives riders a choice of ten calming colored lights.

RANGE ROVER SV AUTOBIOGRAPHY LWB    HOT SUVS

Want comfort? Just push these buttons to get perfect temperature and a comfortable ride.

RANGE ROVER SV AUTOBIOGRAPHY LWB

At the touch of a button, a door opens between the two rear seats to reveal a mini-refrigerator that cools and stores two large bottles plus two glasses.

The Range Rover SV has two touchscreens for rear passengers to access the Internet or watch movies.

RANGE ROVER SV AUTOBIOGRAPHY LWB

# AIR POWER

Range Rover SV Autobiography drivers and passengers breathe easy: the Range Rover uses a special device to cleanse the cabin air. The device breaks the air into electrically charged particles. The particles destroy any airborne **pollutants**.

RANGE ROVER SV AUTOBIOGRAPHY LWB    HOT SUVS

Want to listen to music while breathing in purer air? The Range Rover can deliver the clarity of a live concert with speakers located throughout the cabin.

The Range Rover features 19 speakers strategically placed for surround sound.

Range Rover has a special app that allows owners to control their SUV from a smartphone.

HOT SUVS   RANGE ROVER SV AUTOBIOGRAPHY LWB

# RUGGED RIDE

The Range Rover is designed to work perfectly in water nearly three feet (.91 meters) deep.

Despite its fancy cabin, the Range Rover is rugged. It can plunge through streams, and tackle thick mud, gravel, and deep snow. It can also plow through sandy deserts or chest-high grass. The driver can choose from five driving **modes**.

The Range Rover's All-Terrain Progress Control (ATPC) allows it to operate from an ultra-low "creep" mode at a constant speed of 1.1 miles (1.77 kilometers) per hour when climbing a steep rocky hill, for example. Other modes do the same at higher speeds when ploughing through thick mud or snow. There are even modes for deep sand and other types of difficult driving. In truth, the Range Rover SV Autobiography LWB can go just about anywhere on Earth.

RANGE ROVER SV AUTOBIOGRAPHY LWB    HOT SUVS

The ATPC allows the driver to concentrate on steering the vehicle over and around obstacles, while it automatically keeps a constant speed that may otherwise may be difficult to achieve.

# HOT SUVS  RANGE ROVER SV AUTOBIOGRAPHY LWB

## ALL SEEING

You don't have to strain your eyes or twist your neck when driving a Range Rover. The SUV has a surround-camera system, four digital cameras placed around the vehicle, providing a 360-degree overhead view on the dashboard's touchscreen. The ability to display several views at one time helps with parking and other maneuvers. The reverse camera automatically displays the view behind the vehicle when reverse gear is engaged. When surround view is selected, the images from each camera combine to create an overhead view of the SUV.

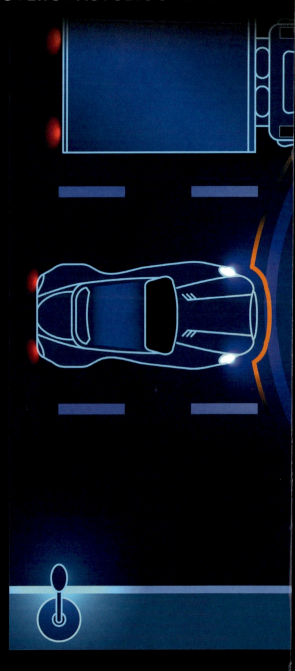

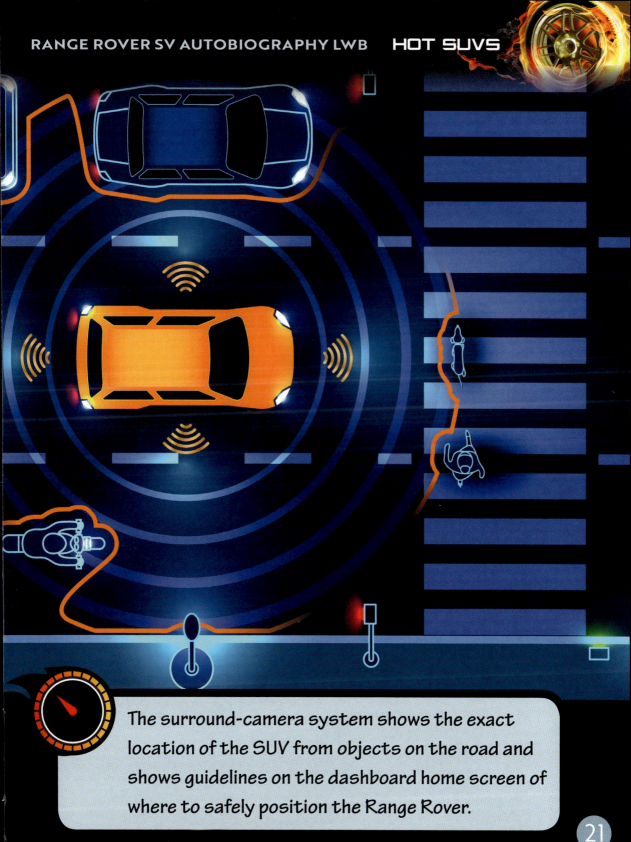

The surround-camera system shows the exact location of the SUV from objects on the road and shows guidelines on the dashboard home screen of where to safely position the Range Rover.

HOT SUVS    RANGE ROVER SV AUTOBIOGRAPHY LWB

# PARKING PRO

The Range Rover SV Autobiography LWB is seven feet (2.13 meters) wide and 18.7 feet (5.7 meters) long. Parking such a large vehicle could be a challenge, but Range Rover makes that relatively easy. **Proximity** sensors use **radar** to tell the Range Rover SV Autobiography LWB driver how close he or she is to a parked car in front and in back. The lane-keeping system instantly senses if the Range Rover SV Autobiography LWB wanders out of its highway lane.

RANGE ROVER SV AUTOBIOGRAPHY LWB    HOT SUVS

Radar is short for radio detection and ranging. Invented in the 1930s, radar sends out pulses of high-frequency waves that are reflected off an object, such as another car, and back to its source.

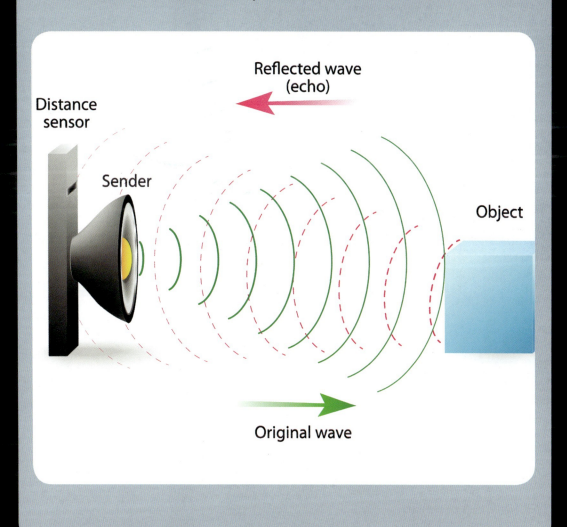

HOT SUVS    RANGE ROVER SV AUTOBIOGRAPHY LWB

# The Range Rover Story

Range Rover developed from Land Rover, the world-famous off-road SUV produced by the Rover car company of Great Britain. Land Rovers got their start in 1948 as the British version of the American Jeep. They quickly became known as an exploration vehicle that could travel across the African plains, the Himalayan mountains, and the Arctic.

During the late 1940s and 1950s, Land Rovers were famous for exploring remote parts of Africa, Latin America, and Asia. The first car people in remote parts of the world may have ever seen was a Land Rover.

## HOT SUVS — RANGE ROVER SV AUTOBIOGRAPHY LWB

The first Range Rover was built in 1970 and quickly evolved into a luxury SUV. In 1979, a Range Rover won the first Paris-Dakar Rally, an endurance race across the Sahara Desert. Beginning in 1994, Range Rover concentrated on comfort—providing owners with the most amazing luxury while keeping the SUV capable of tackling the most extreme off-road adventures.

The 1970 Range Rover could go anywhere, even in a rushing stream.

## HOT SUVS — RANGE ROVER SV AUTOBIOGRAPHY LWB

The P400e will reach a top speed of 85 miles (136.8 kilometers) per hour in electric-only mode with a fully charged battery pack.

Range Rover now has an optional voice recognition system that will allow the P400e and other future models to respond to voice commands instead of buttons.

# Electrifying Future

For 2020 and beyond, Range Rover will offer a hybrid gas and electric vehicle, the Range Rover P400e. With 472 pound-feet (640 Newton-meters) of torque, it can reach 60 miles (96.56 kilometers) per hour in 6.4 seconds and can travel as fast as 137 miles (220.5 kilometers) per hour using full hybrid power. The P400e will be even more stylish and luxurious than the SV Autobiography, with wider, softer seats, door-panel controls, and improved massage functions.

## GLOSSARY

**cargo** (KAHR-goh): freight carried by a ship, plane, truck, or other vehicle

**horsepower** (HORS-pou-ur): a unit for measuring the power of an engine

**modes** (mohds): particular ways of doing something

**pollutants** (puh-LOO-tuhnts): harmful substances

**proximity** (prahk-SIM-i-tee): nearness in space, time, or relationship

**radar** (RAY-dahr): a way ships, planes, and other vehicles find solid objects by reflecting radio waves off them and by receiving the reflected waves

**stylish** (STY-lish): displaying the latest style, fashionable

**terrain** (tuh-RAYN): a particular area of land

**torque** (tork): a twisting force that causes rotation

## INDEX

ATPC  18
battery pack  29
cabin  8, 14, 16
climate control zone  10
Dakar Rally  26
engine  6
Internet  12
Land Rover  24
long wheel base  5
P400e  29
Sahara Desert  26
speakers  15
surround-camera system  20, 21
touchscreen  20

## SHOW WHAT YOU KNOW

1. What does "SV" stand for in Range Rover SV?
2. What is the main advantage of four climate-control zones?
3. How many digital cameras does the Range Rover SV Autobiography have?
4. Where does the Dakar Rally take place?
5. When was the first Range Rover built?

## FURTHER READING

Arnold, Nick, *How Cars Work: The Interactive Guide to Mechanisms That Make a Car Move*, Running Press, 2013.
Colson, Rob, *Top Marques: SUVs and Off Roaders*: Wayland Publishers, 2016.
Zink, Bradley, *It Starts with a Key: How Cars Work*: CreateSpace Independent Publishing Platform, 2016.

## ABOUT THE AUTHOR

Charles Piddock is the former Editor-in-Chief of Weekly Reader Corporation. He has written many books for both young people and adults. He and his wife live by a lake in south-central Maine.

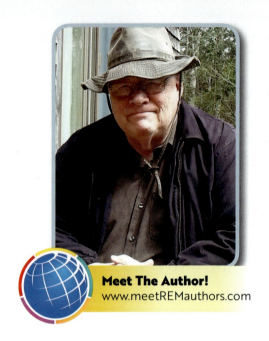

Meet The Author!
www.meetREMauthors.com

© 2019 Rourke Educational Media

All rights reserved. No part of this book may be reproduced or utilized in any form or by any means, electronic or mechanical including photocopying, recording, or by any information storage and retrieval system without permission in writing from the publisher.

www.rourkeeducationalmedia.com

PHOTO CREDITS: All images © landrover.com except cover © Eans; Header art © Petrosg; speedometer art © didis both from Shutterstock.com; page 20-21 © By Andrey Suslov / Shutterstock.com; page 23 © istockphoto

Edited by: Keli Sipperley

Cover design by: Rhea Magaro-Wallace

### Library of Congress PCN Data

Range Rover SV Autobiography LWB / Charles Piddock
 (*VROOM!* Hot SUVs)
  ISBN 978-1-64156-476-2 (hard cover)
  ISBN 978-1-64156-602-5 (soft cover)
  ISBN 978-1-64156-716-9 (e-Book)
Library of Congress Control Number: 2018930696

Rourke Educational Media
Printed in the United States of America, North Mankato, Minnesota